Whales Are AMAZING...
Just Like You!

You ARE AMAZING !
Tony

Written and Illustrated by
Tony Viehmann

depot
PUBLISHING

www.depotpublishing.com   12 Depot Street, Kennebunk, ME 04043
Written, illustrated, published and printed in Maine, USA.
©2016 Tony Viehmann Second Printing

Whales come in all sizes, shapes and colors...
just like you!

The biggest whale of all is the Blue Whale.
It is longer than two school buses!

Whales get hungry
and like to eat...
just like you!

How many fish do you
think it would take to fill this
Sperm Whale's tummy?

Young whales need to stay
close to mom or dad...
just like you!

Mom will stay very protective of her
baby until it can take care of itself.

Whales sing
beautiful songs...
just like you!

Try it!

SQUEAK   GROAN
SNORT
ROAR   MOAN
GRUNT
SNORE

Whales love to
≥ SPLASH... ≤
just like you!

Have you ever done a bellyflop
like this Humpback Whale?

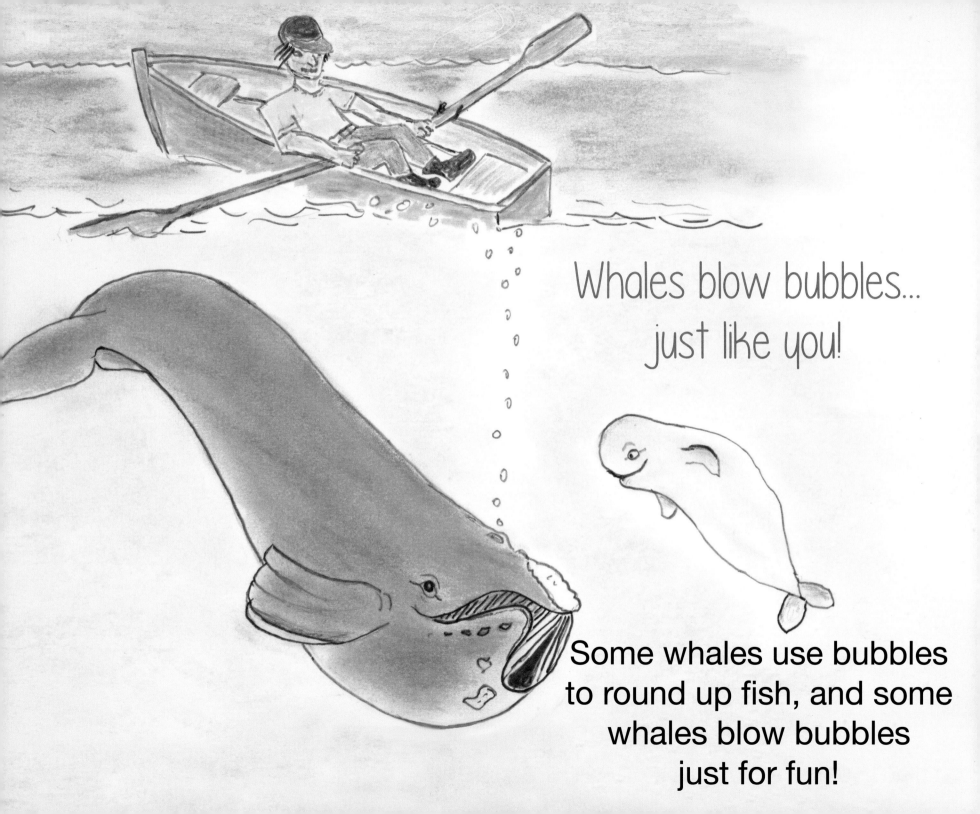

Whales blow bubbles...
just like you!

Some whales use bubbles
to round up fish, and some
whales blow bubbles
just for fun!

Whales get
piggyback rides...
just like you!

Gray whales travel very long
distances. Look who needs a ride!

Whales breathe air...
just like you!

When a baby whale is born, mom gives it a gentle nudge to the surface for its first breath of air.

Whales like to jump
high in the air...
just like you!

Imagine the splash
and the sound when
it lands on the water!

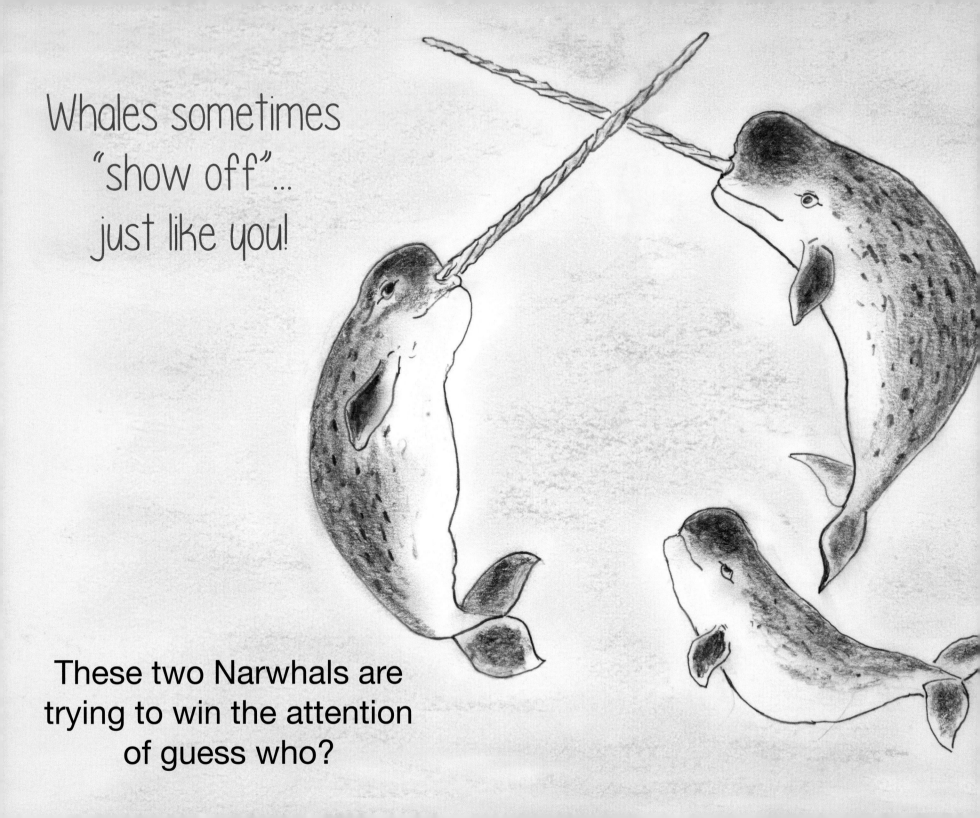

Young whales
have "babysitters"...
just like you!

When mom or dad dives deep for
food, a friend looks after the baby.

Whales get tired and need to rest...
just like you!

This Humpback sleeps with half its brain asleep
and half awake so it will remember to breathe.

Some dolphins can spin
and do somersaults...
just like you!

Imagine how
much fun it would
be to jump out of
the water and
do a somersault
just like this
Spinner dolphin.

Whales like to scratch... just like you!

What a big surprise for the lobsterman!

Whales have unique markings or "fingerprints"... just like you!

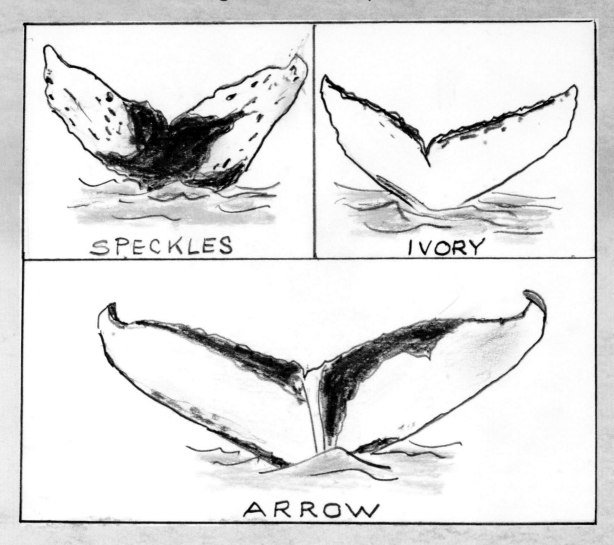

SPECKLES

IVORY

ARROW

Each whale has its own personality, and some whales are even given names.

Whales can be gentle...
just like you!

These Pilot whales are good friends. Whales are sometimes called "gentle giants."

What do you think this "spyhopping"
Humpback is wondering?

Whales sometimes need HELP... just like you!

Whales can get caught up in rope or fishing nets.

Some whales live together in families...
just like you!

Whales have aunts and
uncles and cousins and
even grandparents!

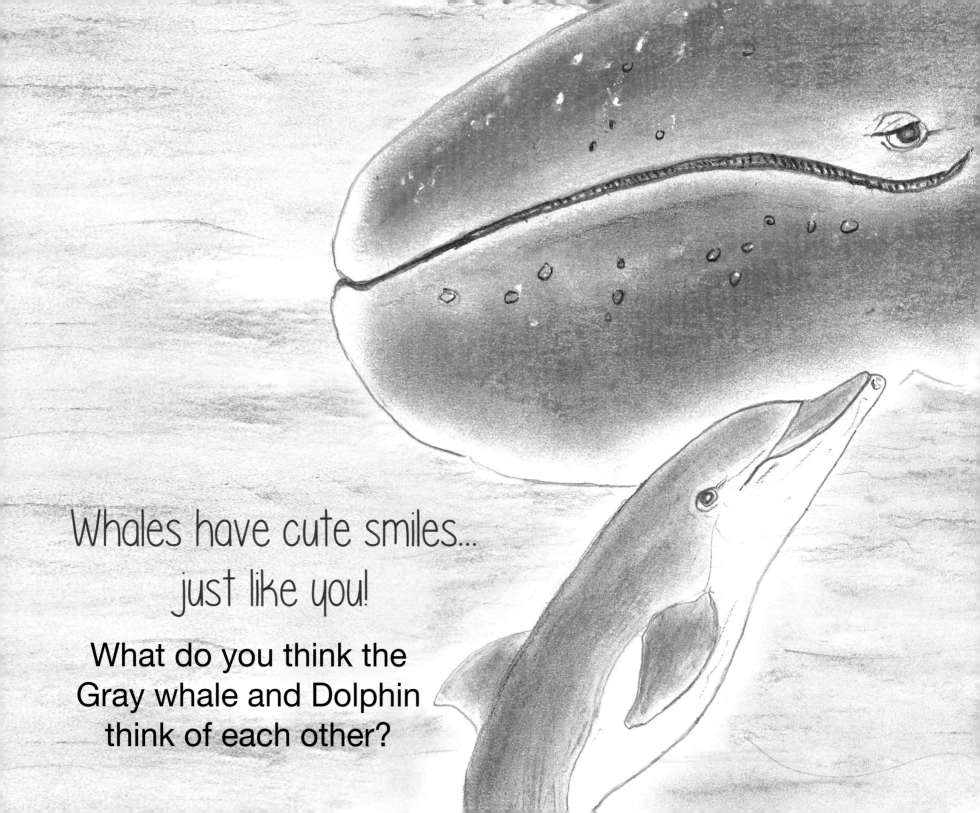

Whales have cute smiles...
just like you!

What do you think the
Gray whale and Dolphin
think of each other?

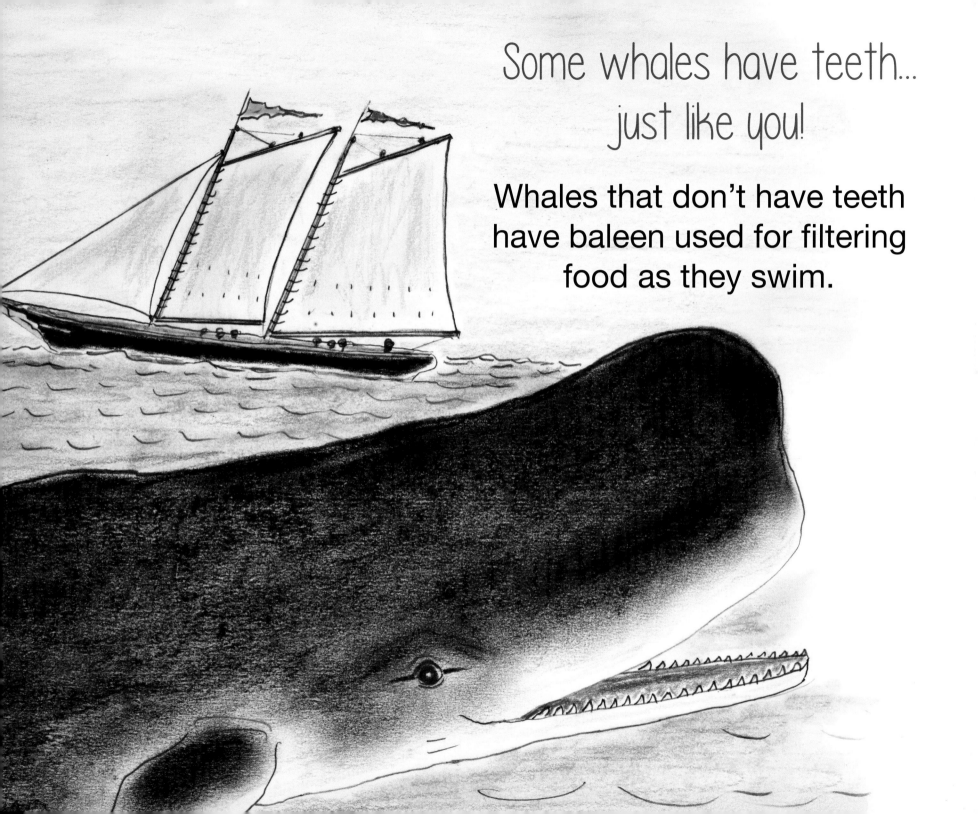

Some whales have teeth...
just like you!

Whales that don't have teeth
have baleen used for filtering
food as they swim.

Whales stay good friends for a very long time... just like you!

If a whale needs help, its friends will stay by its side until help arrives.

Whales are AMAZING...
just like you!

Fun Things To Do!

 Build a dolphin on the beach or in the snow.

 Make pancakes or cookies in the shape of a whale.

 Ask your librarian to help you select a book about whales.

 Practice drawing whales. Use pictures to help.

 Tell your friends all about whales.

 Go on a whale watch! Visit a whale museum.

 Shut your eyes, pretend you're in the sea, and make whale sounds.

Fun Things To Think About!

 Baleen is made out of keratin, just like your fingernails.

 A Blue Whale's heart is the size of a Volkswagen "Punchbuggy."

 A Sperm Whale can hold its breath under water for over an hour.

 A baby Blue Whale drinks up to 100 gallons of milk a day.

 Gray Whales travel from Alaska to Mexico, and back, every year.

 Only the male Narwhal has a six foot tusk which is actually a tooth.

 Whales get straight A's on their report cards for being AMAZING!

A Very Brief History of Whales

1

Fifty million years ago, four legged creatures moved from land to the sea and slowly evolved into whales.

2 Two thousand years ago, whales were misunderstood as monsters of the deep.

3

Thar She BLOWS

1854

For hundreds of years, whales were hunted. The whale oil was used to light lamps.

4 Today, lots of people enjoy looking at whales from whalewatch boats.